This book belongs to

YOU ARE
Three

Sara O'Leary

artwork by

Karen Klassen

Owlkids Books

So much has changed in just a year.

You are three!

We used to always know
where to find you.

But now you are here,
there, and everywhere.

Three is a busy age, and you are
the busiest of bees.
Every day holds some
new discovery.

Your stuffed animals are characters
        in your games of make-believe.
And you are constantly
        coming to their rescue.

Our little hero.

You can name colors
and shapes
now that you are three.

You make pictures of what you see
so that we can see it, too.

Now that you are three,
you love to say your ABCs.

You have little friends now, and you
can tell when they want to play a game.

And when they need a hug.

Now that you are three, you understand
what some, more, and all mean.

You prefer all.

You are still our baby
but you are also your own person.

We love to hold you close
and we love to watch you run.

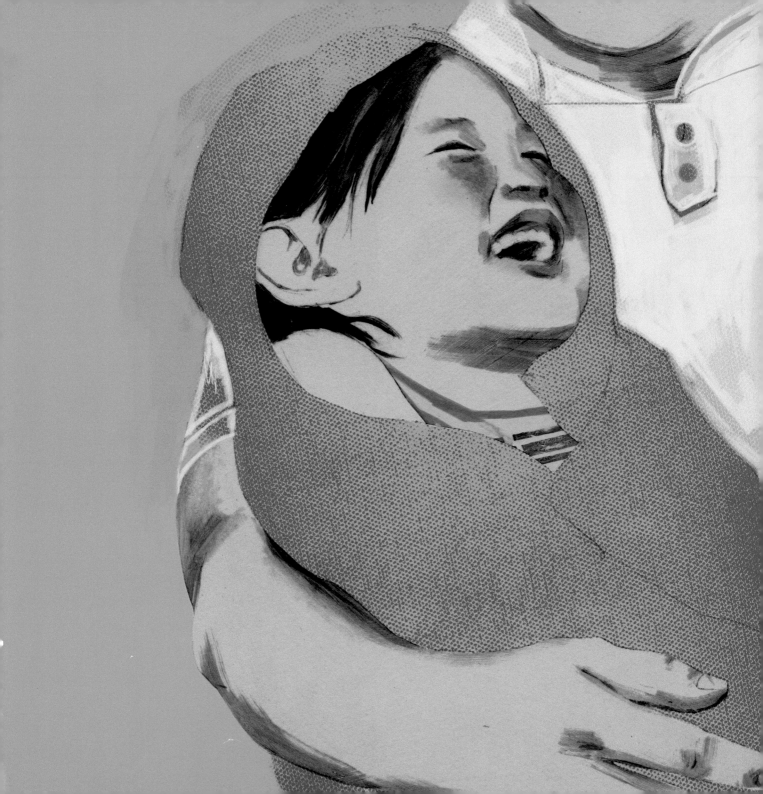

We have conversations now.

You tell us all about your day
and all the things you've done.

You are three,
and everything is changing so quickly.
But what will never, ever change
is our love for you.

Owlkids Books acknowledges the financial support of the Canada Council for the Arts, the Ontario Arts Council, the Government of Canada through the Canada Book Fund (CBF) and the Government of Ontario through the Ontario Media Development Corporation's Book Initiative for our publishing activities.

Published in Canada by
Owlkids Books Inc.
10 Lower Spadina Avenue
Toronto, ON M5V 2Z2

Published in the United States by
Owlkids Books Inc.
1700 Fourth Street
Berkeley, CA 94710

Library and Archives Canada Cataloguing in Publication

O'Leary, Sara, author
        You are three / written by Sara O'Leary ; artwork by Karen Klassen.

(You are ; 3)
ISBN 978-1-77147-074-2 (hardback)

        I. Klassen, Karen, 1977-, illustrator II. Title.

PS8579.L293Y688 2017   jC813'.54   C2016-904926-4

Library of Congress Control Number: 2016946921

The text is set in Clarendon LT Std.
Edited by: Jennifer Stokes and Sarah Howden
Designed by: Alisa Baldwin

ONTARIO ARTS COUNCIL
CONSEIL DES ARTS DE L'ONTARIO
an Ontario government agency
un organisme du gouvernement de l'Ontario

Canada Council   Conseil des Arts
for the Arts   du Canada

Canadä

Manufactured in Shenzhen, Guangdong, China, in November 2016, by WKT Co. Ltd.
Job #16B1430

A   B   C   D   E   F

Publisher of Chirp, chickaDEE and OWL
www.owlkidsbooks.com

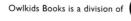 Owlkids Books is a division of Bayard
CANADA